Peter Collington

A Small Miracle

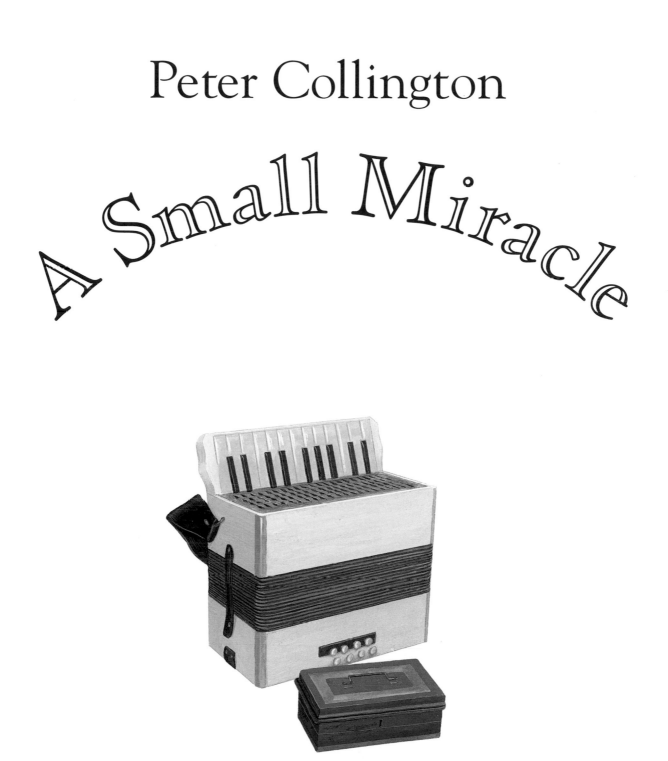

Alfred A. Knopf

NEW YORK

THIS IS A BORZOI BOOK PUBLISHED BY ALFRED A. KNOPF, INC.

First American edition, 1997
Copyright © 1997 by Peter Collington
All rights reserved under International and Pan-American Copyright Conventions.
Published in the United States by Alfred A. Knopf, Inc., New York,
and simultaneously in Canada by Random House of Canada Limited, Toronto.
Distributed by Random House, Inc., New York.
Published in Great Britain in 1997
by Jonathan Cape Children's Books Limited, London.

http://www.randomhouse.com/

Library of Congress Cataloging-in-Publication Data

Collington, Peter. A small miracle / Peter Collington.
p.   cm.
Summary: The figures in a Nativity scene come to life to help an old woman in
need at Christmas.
ISBN 0-679-88725-3
[1. Christmas—Fiction. 2. Crèches (Nativity scenes)—Fiction.
3. Stories without words.] I. Title.
PZ7.C686Sm 1997
[E]—dc21
96-53916

Printed in Hong Kong

10 9 8 7 6 5 4 3 2 1

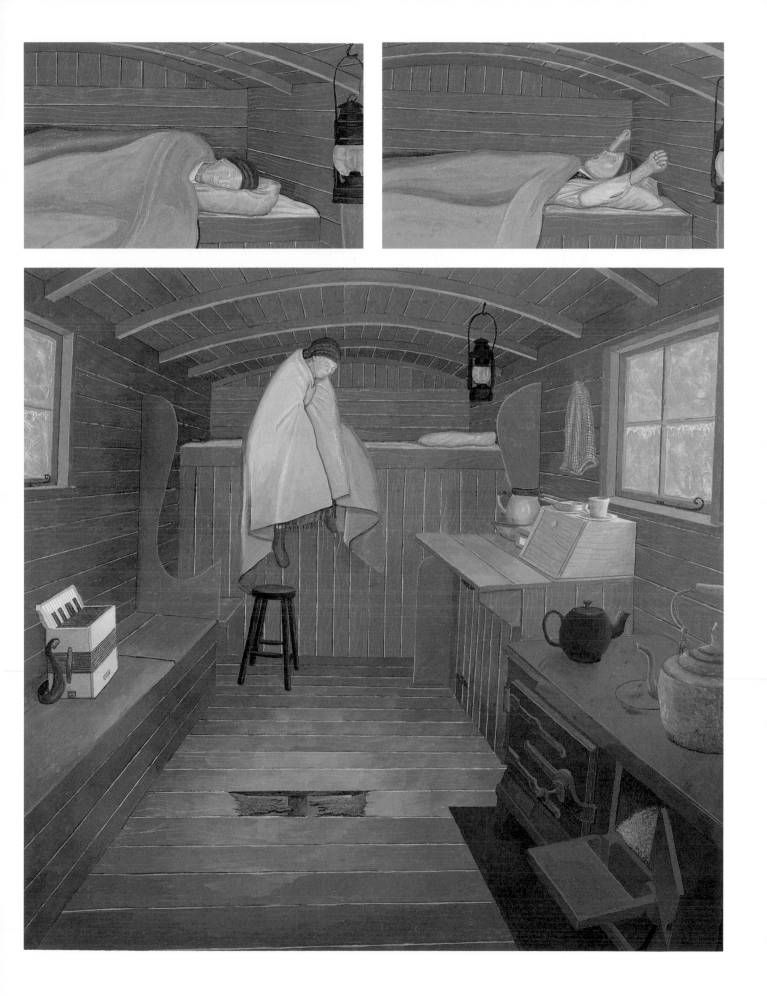

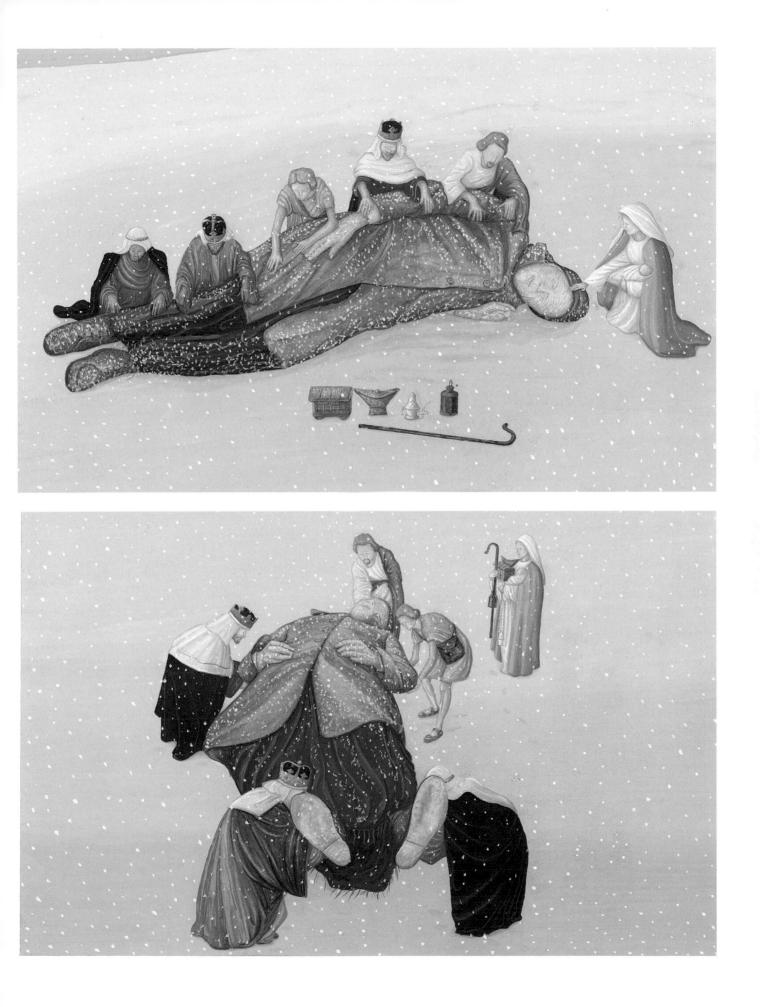

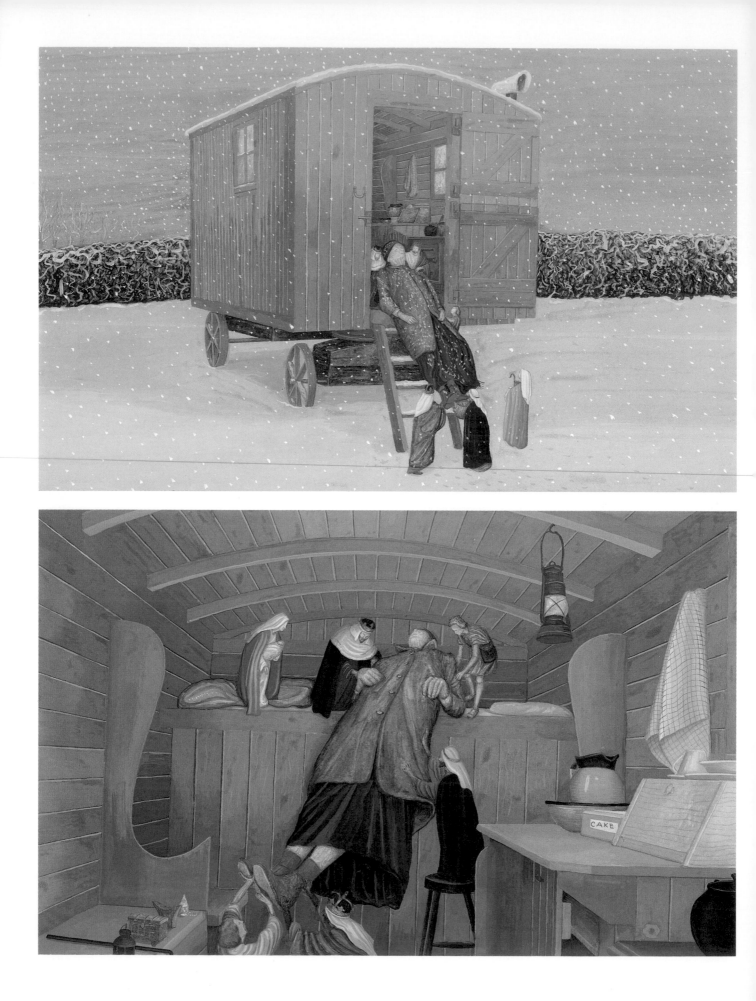

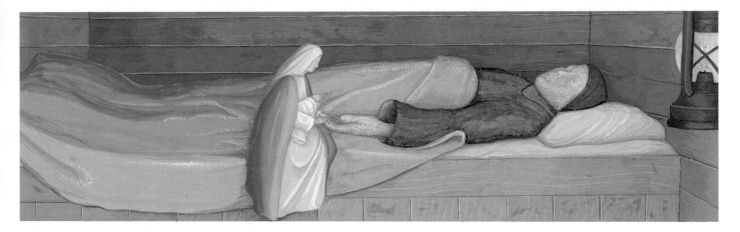

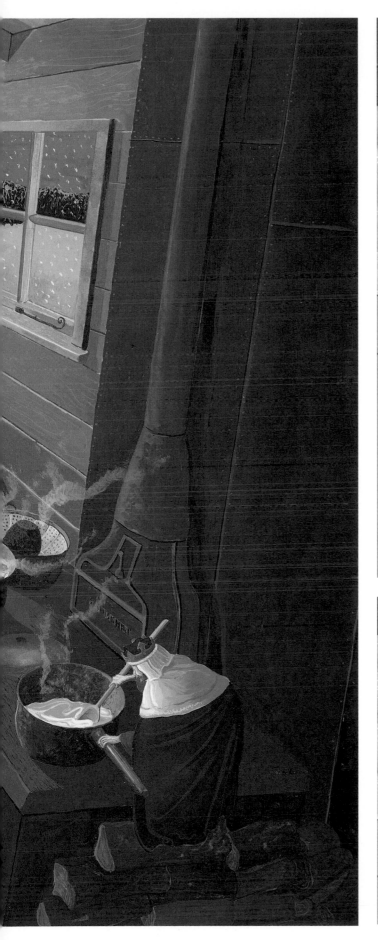

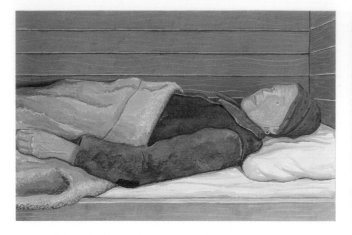